A Note to Parents

For many children, learning math
math!" is their first response — to which ...
add "Me, too!" Children often see adults comfortably reading
and writing, but they rarely have such models for mathematics. And math fear can be catching!

The easy-to-read stories in this **Hello Math** series were written to give children a positive introduction to mathematics,
and parents a pleasurable re-acquaintance with a subject
that is important to everyone's life. **Hello Math** stories make
mathematical ideas accessible, interesting, and fun for children. The activities and suggestions at the end of each book
provide parents with a hands-on approach to help children
develop mathematical interest and confidence.

Enjoy the mathematics!
• Give your child a chance to retell the story. The more famil-
iar children are with the story, the more they will understand
its mathematical concepts.
• Use the colorful illustrations to help children "hear and see"
the math at work in the story.
• Treat the math activities as games to be played for fun.
Follow your child's lead. Spend time on those activities that
engage your child's interest and curiosity.
• Activities, especially ones using physical materials, help
make abstract mathematical ideas concrete.

Learning is a messy process. Learning about math calls for
children to become immersed in lively experiences that help
them make sense of mathematical concepts and symbols.

Although learning about numbers is basic to math, other
ideas, such as identifying shapes and patterns, measuring,
collecting and interpreting data, reasoning logically, and
thinking about chance, are also important. By reading these
stories and having fun with the activities, you will help your
child enthusiastically say **"Hello, Math,"** instead of "I hate
math."

—Marilyn Burns
National Mathematics Educator
Author of *The I Hate Mathematics! Book*

For Bonnie Dry, who always knows what time it is

— T.S.

ISBN 0-590-54082-3

Copyright © 1996 by Scholastic Inc.
The activities on pages 27-32 copyright © 1996 by Marilyn Burns.
All rights reserved. Published by Scholastic Inc.
CARTWHEEL BOOKS and the CARTWHEEL BOOKS logo
are registered trademarks of Scholastic Inc.
HELLO MATH READER and the HELLO MATH READER logo
are trademarks of Scholastic Inc.

Library of Congress Cataloging-in-Publication Data

Slater, Teddy.
    Just a minute! / by Teddy Slater; illustrated by Dana Regan; math activities
by Marilyn Burns.
        p.   cm. — (Hello math reader. Level 2)
    Summary: A young boy learns how important it is to know just how long a
minute is. Includes a section with related activities.
    ISBN 0-590-54082-3 (pb)
    [1. Time — Fiction.] I. Regan, Dana, ill. II. Burns, Marilyn, 1941-
III. Title. IV. Series.
PZ7.S6294Ju 1996
[E] — dc20

96-14842
CIP
AC

12 11 10 9 8 7 6 5 4 3 2 1   6 7 8 9/9 0 1/0

Printed in the U.S.A.   24

First Scholastic printing, August 1996

Just a Minute!

by Teddy Slater
Illustrated by Dana Regan

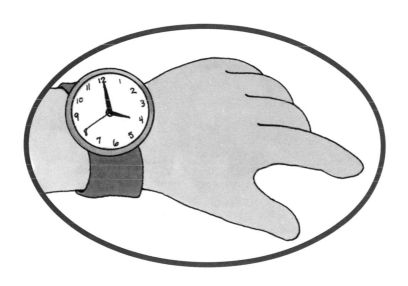

Hello Math Reader — Level 2

SCHOLASTIC INC.

Cartwheel
·B·O·O·K·S·®

New York Toronto London Auckland Sydney

One day, Fred painted
a picture of his family.
He could hardly wait
to show it to them.

Fred's mom was at her computer.
"Look what I did!" Fred said.
"Just a minute, Fred,"
his mother said.
"I'll be right with you."

"Have an oatmeal cookie
while you're waiting,"
she added.

Fred went to the kitchen
and ate a cookie.
Then he ate another one.
And another.

Fred washed the cookies down
with a glass of milk.
Then he ate an apple.
And some raisins.

When he finished eating,
Fred went back to the den.
His mom was still working.
So he went to find his dad.

Fred's dad was in the garden.
"Guess what I made!" Fred said.
"Just a minute, Fred,"
his dad said.
"I'm watering the flowers."

Fred watched his father
for a while.
Then he went to his room
and took out his blocks.

Fred built a skyscraper.
Then he built a fort.
And a big castle
with two towers
and a bridge.

When he finished building,
Fred went outside again.
His dad was still watering.
So Fred went to look
for his brothers.

Fred's brothers and their
friends were playing football.
"Sam! Paul!" Fred said. "Look!"
"Just a minute, Fred,"
his brothers said.
"The game is almost over."

Fred watched
his brother Paul
pass the ball.
He watched his brother Sam
catch the ball.

The game went on and on.
And on....
Fred finally gave up
and went back inside.

Just before dinner,
Paul knocked on Fred's door.
"Hey, Fred," he called.
"It's your turn to walk the dog.
Rags needs to go out now."

Fred looked up from his book.
"Just a minute," he said.
"I want to read this page."

Fred read that page.
And the next one.
And the next.
When he finished the book,
he went down to walk Rags.

Fred found his brother Paul
mopping up the big puddle
that the little dog
had just made
on the kitchen floor.

"What took you so long?"
Paul scolded Fred.
"I told you Rags had to go!"
"But I only read for a
minute," Fred
answered.

"That was longer than
a minute," Sam added.
Fred was confused.
"Well, what *is* a minute?"
he asked.

A minute is how long it takes to count, "One 1,000, two 1,000," all the way to "sixty 1,000."

Or, "One Mississippi, two Mississippi," all the way to "sixty Mississippi."

A minute is 60 seconds. That's how long it takes the big second hand on my watch to go around once.

From then on, Fred knew
just how long a minute was.

And his whole family knew
better than to say, "Just a minute,"
unless they really meant it!

• ABOUT THE ACTIVITIES •

Children hear references to time all day long: "Get dressed quickly. We have to be on time!" "You'll have time to play later." "It's time to clean your room." "It's almost bedtime." But time is a complicated idea for children to understand because it's used in many different contexts. For example, we use time to talk about how long things take: The cookies need to bake for 15 minutes. We also use time to define a specific moment: The bus comes at 7:20. Sometimes it's important to be accurate about time: The movie starts in 5 minutes. Sometimes we just estimate: I'll be ready in 5 minutes or so. Children need many experiences to understand all the different ways we talk about time.

Learning to tell time on clocks and watches is also complicated. In part, this is because of the wide variety of timekeepers children see. Digital clocks and watches display digits to show times, while analog clocks and watches rely on the position of the hands. Also, there are many different kinds of analog timekeepers. Some have three hands, and some have only two. Some show regular numbers, others use Roman numerals, and some don't have any numbers at all.

When children see the benefits of being able to tell time and want to learn to do so, then it's time to help them get started. As with all learning, your child's interest holds an important key. The activities in this section give children first-hand experience with one specific measure of time: a minute. These activities engage your child (and you) in thinking about how long a minute really is. The directions are written for you to read along with your child. Follow your child's interests and enjoy the math!

— Marilyn Burns

You'll find tips and suggestions
for guiding the activities whenever
you see a box like this!

Retelling the Story

When Fred wanted to show his painting to his mom, she said, "Just a minute." What do you think she was telling Fred?

Fred ate cookies. He drank a glass of milk. Then he ate an apple and some raisins. About how long do you think it would take Fred to do all that?

When Fred wanted to show his painting to his dad, his dad said, "Just a minute." What do you think he was telling Fred?

Fred took out his blocks. He built a skyscraper, a fort, and then a castle. Do you think Fred played with the blocks for a long time or a short time?

Fred watched his brothers play football. How long do you think he watched them play?

Back in his room, Fred finished reading a book. About how long do you think it took him?

How Long Is a Minute?

Here are some ways to feel how long a minute is. For each, someone will say "start" to start timing one minute, and then say "one minute" after a minute passes. During that time, try doing one of the things listed below. Start again and try another.

Close your eyes and keep them closed for one minute.

Clap your hands for one minute.

Try standing on one foot for a minute.

You can also make up some other things to try.

Counting a Minute

How high do you think you can count in one minute? Try it while someone else keeps time.

At the end of the story, Sam and Paul give Fred hints about ways to count so that it takes one minute to get to 60. That's because they knew that there are 60 seconds in a minute.

Paul counted, "One 1,000, two 1,000, . . ."
Sam counted, "One Mississippi, two Mississippi, . . ."

Try counting these ways while someone else keeps time. See how close you get to 60 in one minute.

Don't worry about whether or not your child gets exactly to 60. With practice, counting will become more useful as a way to time one minute.

More or Less

Here are some things you do every day. For each one, guess whether you think it takes more than a minute or less than a minute to do it. Now try each thing while someone keeps time.

Put on your socks and shoes.

Brush your teeth.

Eat a cookie or a banana.

Now make up things of your own to try that you think would take about one minute.

One-Minute Stars

How many stars do you think you could draw in one minute? Get a piece of paper and a pencil and try it while someone times you. Then count and see how many you drew.

It doesn't matter what kind of star your child draws. Also, counting may be difficult with stars scattered all over the page. To help keep track, have your child write numbers over each star as she or he counts.

Try the same game again, but draw something different. You might draw little triangles or dollar signs, or see how many times you can write your name in one minute.